The
TALLEST
of
smalls

To

From

Date

The TALLEST of smalls

Max Lucado

Illustrated by **Maria Monescillo**

Tommy NELSON®

A Division of Thomas Nelson Publishers

NASHVILLE   MEXICO CITY   RIO DE JANEIRO

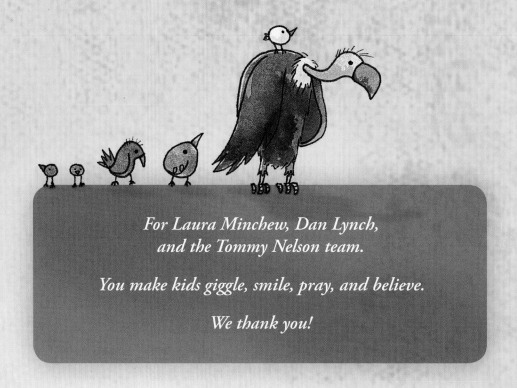

For Laura Minchew, Dan Lynch,
and the Tommy Nelson team.

You make kids giggle, smile, pray, and believe.

We thank you!

The TALLEST of smalls

Text and Illustrations © 2009 by Max Lucado.

Illustrations by Maria Monescillo
Karen Hill, executive editor to Max Lucado

Published in Nashville, Tennessee, by Tommy Nelson. Tommy Nelson is a registered trademark of Thomas Nelson, Inc.

Thomas Nelson, Inc., titles may be purchased in bulk for educational, business, fund-raising, or sales promotional use. For information, please e-mail SpecialMarkets@ThomasNelson.com.

Cover, interior design, and art direction by Koechel Peterson & Associates, Minneapolis, MN.

ISBN 978-1-4003-1514-7

Library of Congress Cataloging-in-Publication Data
Lucado, Max.
  The Tallest of Smalls / Max Lucado ; illustrations by Maria Monescillo.
      p. cm.
  Summary: A rhyming story about how Jesus can lift up even those who feel small and worthless.
  ISBN 978-1-4003-1514-7 (hardback) [1. Stories in rhyme. 2. Christian life—Fiction. 3. Self-esteem—Fiction.]
I. Monescillo, Maria, ill. II. Title.
  PZ8.3.L9615Tal 2009
  [E] —dc22

                                                    2009011435

Printed in China

17 18 19 DSC 10 9 8 7
Mfr: DSC | Shenzhen, China | March 2017-PPO# 9438990

Dear Parent,

What do you do when your child feels small and insignificant? What do you say to smooth the hurt feelings? What does your child need from you?

Here's a hint: Think about what you need from your heavenly Father when you feel small and insignificant. You need a reminder.

A reminder that you're loved.

A reminder that you're special.

A reminder that what your heavenly Father thinks of you trumps what the world might say.

And a reminder that your Father would move heaven and earth to have you near Him. (He did.)

A few reminders can mend scraped knees and bruised feelings.

A hug won't hurt, either.

Blessings,
Max Lucado

Perhaps you don't know—

then, maybe you do—

the **Too Smalls** of Stiltsville

and their story for you,

where people like we—
some tiny, **some tall,**
with games and schools
and clocks on the wall—

keep an eye on the time,
for each **evening** at **six**,
they meet in the circle
for the **purpose** of **sticks**;

tall stilts upon which a Stiltsvillian can **strut**

and be lifted **above** those down in the **rut**.

the **less** and
the **least**,
the **shy** and **shier**,

the **not**-cools
and have-**nots**

who want to **go higher**

but **can't** because in the **giving of sticks,** their names are **not** called; they **NEVER** get picked.

Like **Ollie,** the boy
whose **pants** have a **patch,**
whose **legs** are too **skinny;**
his socks never match.

He **laughs** with a **snort** and **sleeps** with a **drool**, too common and **dull** for the **gang** of the **cool**,

who **decides** who is **special**,
who's **in** and who's **out**,

who's **better**, who's **best**,
and declares with **a shout**,

"You're **awesome!**" "You're **pretty!**"
"You're **clever**" or "**Funny!**"
And gives out a **prize**—
not of **medals** or **money**,

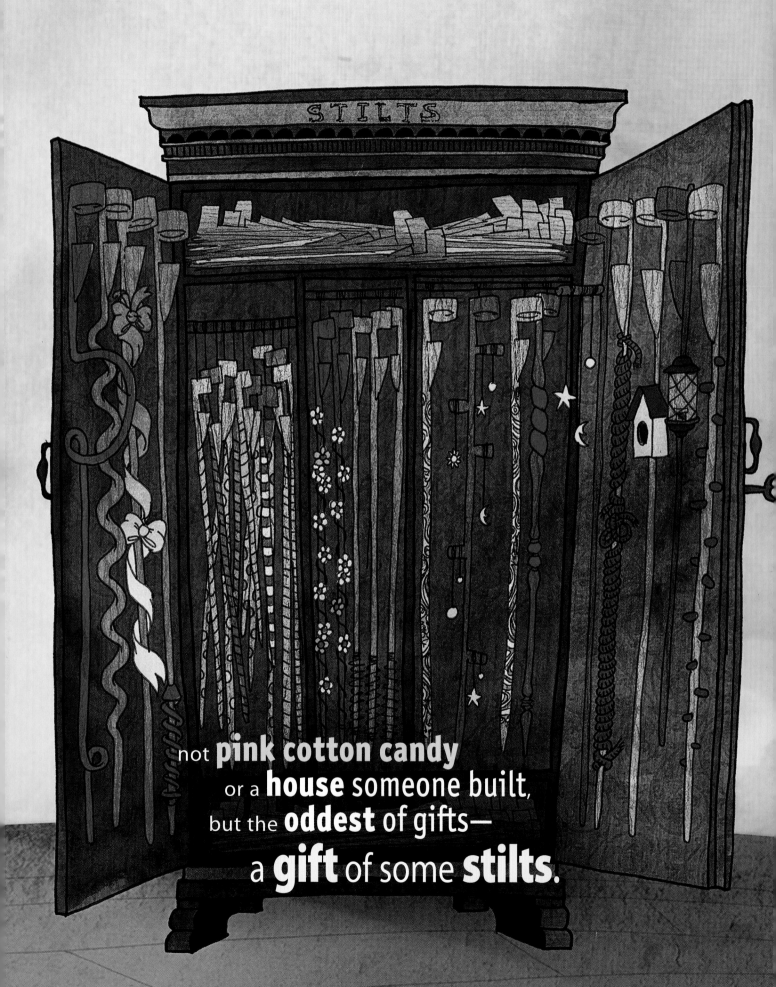

not **pink cotton candy**
or a **house** someone built,
but the **oddest** of gifts—
a **gift** of some **stilts**.

Ollie wanted those **stilts**
so much he would **plea**
from the **midst** of the **crowd**,

"Pick me!
Please, pick me!"

And one night to **Ollie's surprise,** they did.

"**You're cool!**" they declared.

"**Hip-hip, hip, hooray!**"

"**Come up** to the **front,**
for this is **your day**

to join the **classy** and **sassy** and **move** up the **ladder.**"
When they **lifted him up,** he knew that **he mattered.**

He **looked down** from **above**,
he **looked down** his **nose**

at the **common**, the **plain**.
Yes, he **smirked** as he **rose**.

But his smile **didn't last**,
for soon **he discovered**
that **birds** like to **perch**,

and **soon**
he was **covered**...

with pigeons and buzzards
and all flying things;
they **plopped** on his **shoulders**
and rested their wings

while he struggled to **walk**
and **maintain** some balance.

"Do I *have* this **skill**?
Do I *have* this **talent**?"

Ollie **reached** for the sky
with a **tilt** and a **sway**.
"Look out below!"
He fell **straight away**

into the **Too Smalls,**
right back where he started
among the **stiltless** and **small**;
and oh **how it smarted**…

when the **gang** of the **cool**, in the **jilt** of all **jilts**, didn't offer to **help**. They just **took** his **stilts**. And there **Ollie sat**.

He might not have **moved**,
might have **sat** there and **cried**,
except for the **touch** he
felt on his **side**...

so gentle, so caring,
that he looked up to see
Jesus smile down and say,
"Ollie, come walk with me.

"**Keep your feet on the ground,**
refuse to be stilted;
choose low over high;
leave the system tip-tilted.

"You're precious, my Ollie,
not too short or too small;
I made you, remember,
you're mine after all."

So Ollie went home, took the **clock** off the **wall**, enough of the **stilts**, enough of **it all**!

"I may not be much—
the **smallest** of Smalls—
but since **Jesus loves me,**
I'm the **tallest** of talls."